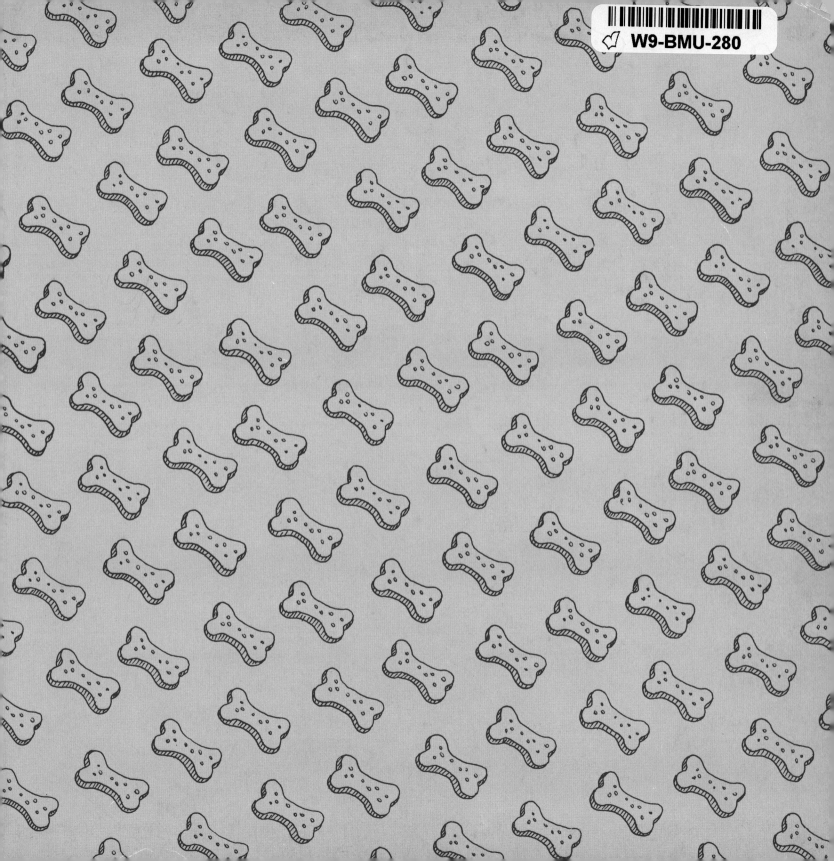

This book belongs to

_MK_

Spunky's™ Camping Adventure
Copyright © 1998
Global Television Syndications
Christian Broadcasting Network

Published by Bethany House Publishers under license from Bethel Publishing, publisher of *Spunky's Diary* by Janette Oke. This story was adapted for television by Patrick Granleese and modified for print by Sue & Lorianne Wilkinson. Illustrated by Elizabeth Gatt., Sue Wilkinson, and Holly Lennox. Art Direction by Angela Ward Costello, Lindy Lindstrom, Sue Wilkinson, Dynomight Cartoons, and CBN Animation.

Printed in Italy.
Library of Congress Cataloging-in-Publications Data
CIP Data applied for

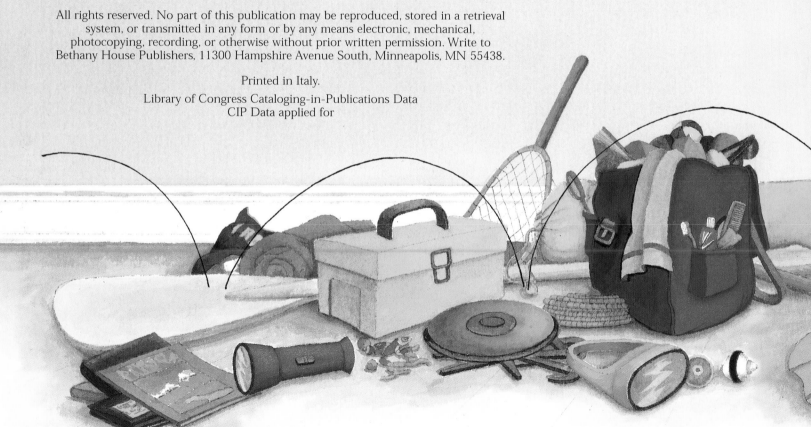

Based on character and story by

JANETTE OKE

Spunky's
CAMPING ADVENTURE

Spunky has hidden his toy ball somewhere on each double page. Can you find it?

*O*h boy! My first camping trip with my master, Mark, and his parents, Mr. and Mrs. Dobson. Spunky left them all setting up the camp and raced around, trying to see and smell everything at once.

There was a rocky lakeshore to investigate, as well as tall trees, all sorts of bushes, funny-smelling flowers, lots and lots of birds, and a huge trailer parked next to their spot. Spunky just knew he was going to love camping!

Spunky returned to find Mark and his parents talking to some people. Mark introduced Spunky to their neighbors, Mr. and Mrs. Johnson, their son, Buzz, and Buzz's dog, Snapper.

Snapper greeted Spunky with a nasty snarl and then crushed a can in his jaws.

Buzz laughed when Spunky hid behind Mark.

Buzz laughed again when he collapsed Mark's tent.

5

The next morning, Mark went snorkeling and found an arrowhead. But Buzz took it from him . . .

then used his slingshot on everything in the park.

Life with Buzz was off to a rough start!

"It's hard to like Buzz," Mark told his father.

"But you just met him," his father wondered. "What about loving your neighbors like Jesus tells us to do?"

"Jesus never met Buzz!" Mark muttered.

"Or his dog!" growled Spunky.

"I'm going to keep trying to love my neighbor, but it sure is hard," Mark whispered to Spunky.

And I'll try to make friends with my neighbor Snapper, Spunky vowed.

The next day, Snapper told Spunky, "If you want to be my friend, watch for Eagle."

"It sure is better to be friends than enemies, huh, Snapper?" Spunky looked around.

Snapper was already halfway up the cliff where Eagle's nest was perched, and he looked like he was ready for trouble.

"Snapper, no!" barked Spunky as Snapper lunged for Eagle's eggs.

Fortunately, Eagle heard Spunky's barking and made a quick dive for Snapper—just in time to save her eggs.

Spunky barked an apology, "Sorry, ma'am, but Snapper's master forgot to teach him right from wrong."

So far, camping hadn't turned out to be much fun for Spunky or Mark. Maybe hiding would be a good way to deal with their new neighbors.

"Let's hide in here," Mark suggested as he climbed into his dad's canoe.

Just then Buzz and Snapper burst into the clearing.

"Hi, Mark! Want to play?" laughed Buzz as he pushed the canoe off the shore and leapt inside.

Snapper knocked Spunky aside and jumped in beside Buzz.

They're not leaving me! thought Spunky as he raced along the shore after Mark. He made a desperate dash across an overhanging branch and leapt for the canoe.

Thump! He made it!

With Spunky safe in the canoe, Mark helped Buzz paddle across the lake and then down a side river. Suddenly, the canoe started moving faster. Then faster!

And FASTER! Now they were flying down the rocky river.

"Look out!" shouted Mark.

"Ahhhh!" wailed Buzz.

The canoe sailed over a small falls, dumping them all into the cold water.

15

Spunky and Snapper swam for the shore, but Mark and Buzz were swept downstream. Spunky and Snapper raced along the shore, trying to keep up with their masters.

Oh no! Mark and Buzz were heading straight for a dangerous waterfall!

17

Just before he was swept over the edge, Buzz
managed to grab an overhanging branch and
drag himself out of the water.

Whew! thought Spunky. At least Buzz was safe.
But where was Mark?

There he was! He was just about to slip under the branch and over the falls! Buzz lunged for Mark's hand.

"Gotcha. Hang on, buddy," sobbed Buzz.

Both boys hugged the branch tightly.

Mark called to Spunky, "Go get help—and fast!"

Leaving Snapper to watch the boys, Spunky headed for higher ground to see where they were. As Spunky looked out over the trees, the hill beneath his feet suddenly reared up. Spunky slid down the mound—and found himself eye to eye with a huge brown bear!

"Excuse me, do you know the way back to camp?" Spunky asked timidly.

ROOOAR!!!

Yikes! Spunky took off, with the bear right behind him. Just when he thought he'd never get away, Spunky was yanked out of the bear's reach and lifted high above the treetops. It was Eagle!

"Aaaahhh!" Spunky struggled in her clutches. "Please don't eat me, ma'am. I'm in a big hurry. It's an emergency!"

"I know," Eagle reassured Spunky. "I saw the accident. I'm trying to help you like you helped me."

They soared toward the camp. Far below, Spunky saw the park ranger pull a life preserver from the water's edge.

Eagle gently set Spunky down at the campsite just as the ranger arrived. Spunky heard him tell everyone that the boys might be in trouble. Spunky barked and barked to let the ranger know he was right.

"What's up, Spunky? Do you know where the boys are?" asked Mrs. Dobson.

"Yes!" barked Spunky.

Everyone piled into the ranger's jeep and headed back to the river. But the ranger turned the wrong way! Spunky leapt out and led the jeep toward the boys.

He could just hear Mark's voice as he scrambled over the last rock.

"I'm scared, too, but try saying a prayer. It always helps me feel better," Mark said.

Buzz tried. "Dear Lord, I know I don't deserve to be saved, but Mark doesn't deserve to drown. Maybe when you save him, you could save me, too?"

Spunky barked in agreement as the jeep pulled up.

25

The ranger quickly gave the end of a rope to Spunky, who gripped it in his teeth and bravely started out across the branch.

Just as Spunky reached the boys, the branch gave a loud groan.

Then, *CRAAACK*. The branch broke.

Clutching the rope, the boys were swept out over the edge of the falls. They dangled there with Spunky wedged between Mark and Buzz.

"Hold on tight!" called the park ranger as he worked to pull up the rope.

27

The boys gripped the rope and Spunky. They tried not to look down at the rocks far below. Slowly, they were pulled to the shore and safety.

"Way to go!" cheered Mr. Dobson.

"Thank goodness!" sighed Mrs. Johnson.

29

Back in camp, everyone sat around the campfire. The heat felt wonderful. So did the friendship and the feeling of forgiveness Spunky felt for Buzz and Snapper.

"Mark, you never did tell us what happened at the falls today," said Mrs. Dobson.

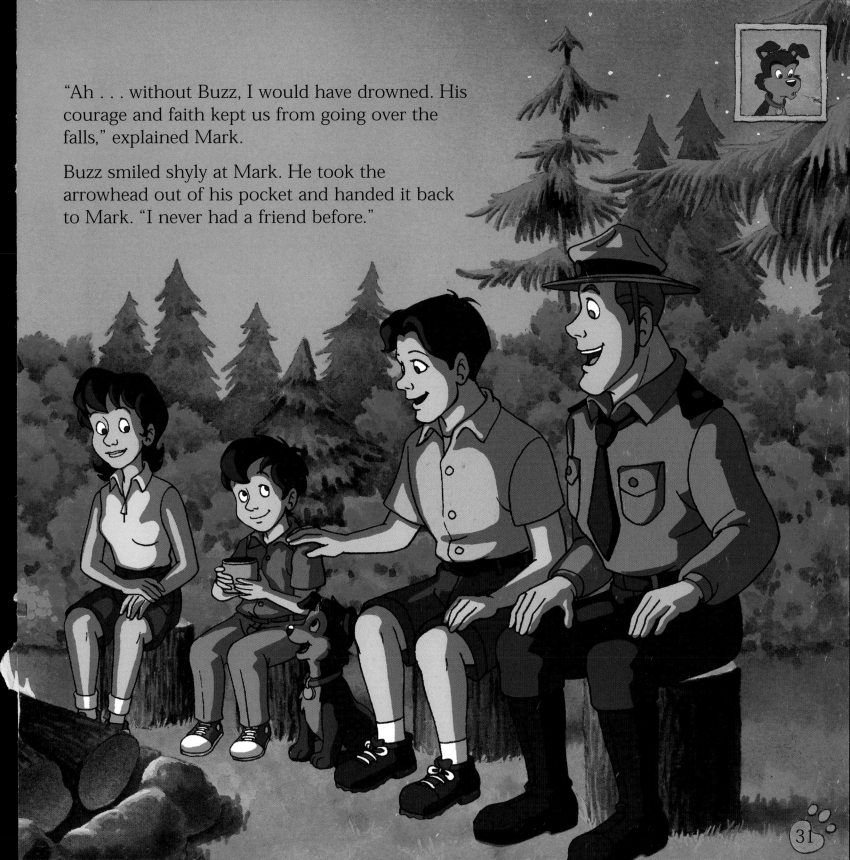

"Ah . . . without Buzz, I would have drowned. His courage and faith kept us from going over the falls," explained Mark.

Buzz smiled shyly at Mark. He took the arrowhead out of his pocket and handed it back to Mark. "I never had a friend before."

Snapper looked at Spunky. "Let's be friends, too."

"Sure!" barked Spunky.

This was going to be a great camping trip after all!

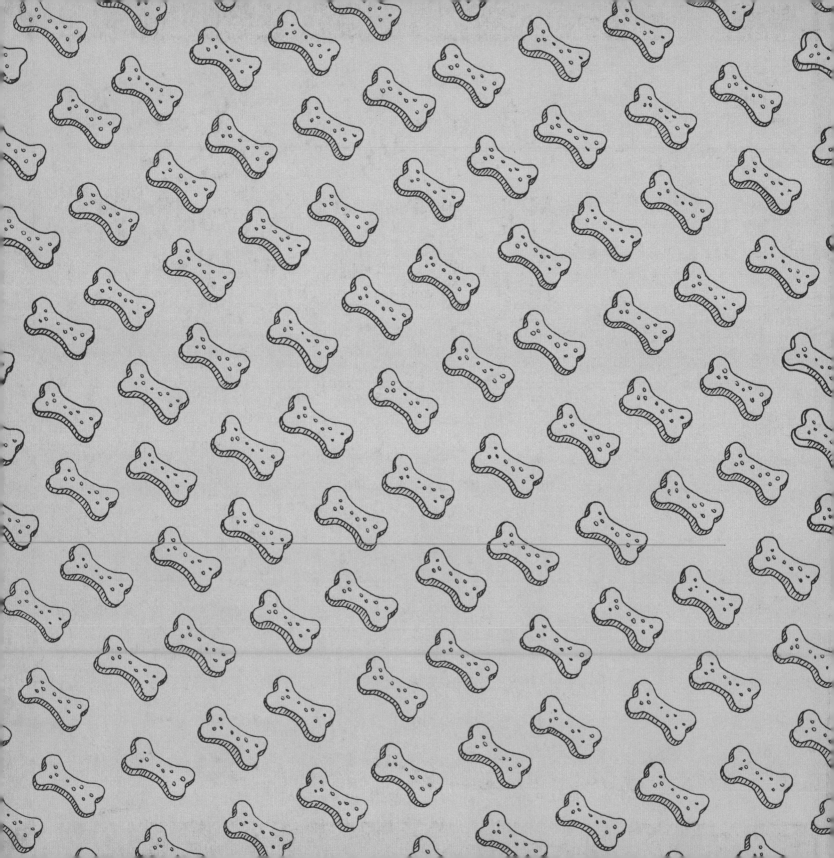